# Grandma Rose's Magic

This
**PJ BOOK**
belongs to

**PJ** Library®

JEWISH BEDTIME STORIES and SONGS

To Grandma Rose, for making magic with her sewing; to my parents, Elaine and Gerry Elovitz, for teaching me the values of hard work and kindness; and to my husband, Bob Marshall, for the joys he brings me—L.E.M.

For Michal with love—A.J.

# Grandma Rose's Magic

Linda Elovitz Marshall

illustrated by
Ag Jatkowska

KAR-BEN
PUBLISHING

With a needle and thread and a piece of cloth, Grandma Rose could make magic.

Grandma Rose made dresses for her daughters and slacks for her sons.

She made blankets for babies,

dolls for grandchildren,

and curtains and quilts for friends and neighbors.

One day, Grandma Rose hemmed a skirt for Mrs. Feldman.

"The hem is perfect," said Mrs. Feldman, "and goodness me, my skirt has beautiful new pink and red buttons shaped like roses."

"Must be magic," answered Grandma Rose.

She put the money Mrs. Feldman paid her into a jar on a shelf in the kitchen.

The next week, Mrs. Cooper visited Grandma Rose.
"My daughter is getting married," she said. "I would
like you to make her a beautiful blue tablecloth."

When the tablecloth was done, Mrs. Cooper came to pick it up. Grandma Rose took the money Mrs. Cooper paid her and put it in the jar.

"The tablecloth is gorgeous," said Mrs. Cooper, "and goodness me, there are also twelve beautiful napkins with borders of blue and gold!"

"Must be magic," answered Grandma Rose.

Grandma Rose sewed a hat for Mrs. Segal,

a scarf for Mrs. Rappaport,

and a shirt for Mr. Cohen.

Whenever Grandma Rose sewed, something magical happened.
Every day she sewed, and every day she saved.

"I am saving my dollars and dimes, my nickels and quarters, and even my pennies," Grandma Rose told her granddaughter Julia. "I am going to buy the most beautiful set of dishes I have ever seen."

"What do they look like?" Julia asked, as Grandma Rose pinned the sleeves on her new dress.

"They look just like the dishes my grandmother used on Shabbos when I was a child," answered Grandma Rose. "Around the edge of every plate and bowl and teacup is a beautiful border of blue and gold, and in the middle of each are pink and red roses."

"Where did you find them?" asked Julia, as Grandma Rose
began to sew.

"Downtown," she answered, "in the big department store."

The money in Grandma Rose's jar grew and grew. When it was full, she counted her dimes, her nickels and quarters, and even her pennies. She had two hundred dollars.

Grandma Rose went to the bank. "I have worked very hard," she told the bank teller. "And now I would like to change my dimes and nickels and quarters and even my pennies into dollars. I am going downtown to buy beautiful dishes with pink and red roses, just like the ones my grandmother had."

"Don't you remember me?" the teller asked. "You made my wonderful wedding dress. And to my surprise, there was also a lacy white wedding veil."

"Must have been magic!" said Grandma Rose.

"It was," said the teller, as she counted out the coins and gave back dollars to Grandma Rose.

But when Grandma Rose got to the store, there was not a single dish with blue and gold trim on the border, and pink and red roses in the middle. Grandma Rose was very sad. She had two hundred dollars in her pocketbook, but she could not set her table with dollar bills.

I don't have my new dishes, she thought, but I can fill my old dishes with good food. So Grandma Rose used some of her money to buy roast beef and turkey, poppy seed rolls, chocolate cookies, and fresh fruit.

When she got home, her sons and daughters, their wives and husbands, and all of her grandchildren were there. Mrs. Feldman and Mrs. Cooper were there. Mrs. Segal, Mr. Cohen, and Mrs. Rappaport were there. Even the bank teller was there.

"Surprise!" they shouted. And in their hands, each person held a plate or a bowl or a teacup with blue and gold trim and a pink and red rose in the middle.

"Thank you," said Mrs. Cooper, as she set a dinner plate on Grandma Rose's dining room table, "for surprising me with a baby blanket when my son was born."

"Thank you," said Mrs. Feldman, as she set a teacup next to the dinner plate, "for surprising me with curtains for my new house."

"Thank you, thank you, thank you," said Mrs. Rappaport, Mr. Cohen, the bank teller, and all the people in her living room, "for making skirts and shirts, blankets and bedspreads, and most of all for bringing us together."

And as Grandma Rose watched her friends and family fill the beautiful new dishes with roast beef and turkey, fancy breads and fruit, she remembered every shirt and skirt and tablecloth and curtain she had made. And she remembered the meals she had shared with her own grandparents so long ago. "Now," she said, "let's eat!

"Look at all this food," said Mr. Cohen. "How did you know we'd all be here?"

"Must be magic," answered Grandma Rose.

**Linda Elovitz Marshall** raised her four children, a small flock of sheep, lots of zucchinis and countless rabbits on a farm in a historic farmhouse overlooking the Hudson River in upstate New York. A graduate of Barnard College of Columbia University, she has taught early childhood and parenting education, owned a bookstore, taught English to people from other countries, and invented giftware. She is also the author of *Talia and the Rude Vegetables*.

**Ag Jatkowska** was born in Gdansk, Poland and grew up by the cold Baltic Sea. She graduated from the Academy of Fine Arts in Gdansk with an M.A. in Graphic Design and Illustration. She is inspired by the way book illustrations can change the way children see the world by stimulating their imaginations. She lives in Bath, England.

Text copyright ©2012 by Linda Elovitz Marshall
Illustrations copyright ©2012 by Ag Jatkowska

KAR-BEN Publishing
A division of Lerner Publishing Group, Inc.
241 First Avenue North
Minneapolis, MN 55401 U.S.A.
800-4KARBEN

Website address: www.karben.com

Library of Congress Cataloging-in-Publication Data

Marshall, Linda Elovitz.
    Grandma Rose's magic / by Linda Elovitz Marshall ; illustrated by Ag Jatkowska.
        p.   cm.
    Summary: Every day Grandma Rose sews for her friends and neighbors and puts away the money she earns, saving for a set of dishes just like her grandmother's Shabbos dishes.
    ISBN 978-0-7613-5215-0 (lib. bdg. : alk. paper)
    [1. Sewing—Fiction. 2. Grandmothers—Fiction. 3. Generosity—Fiction. 4. Jews—Fiction.] I. Jatkowska, Ag, ill. II. Title.
    PZ7.M35672453Gr 2012
    [E]—dc23                                        2011014423

Manufactured in China
2-42260-17615-5/20/2016

201625K/B0941/Grandparent